Wishing on Water

Liz Ashlee

Wishing on Water
Copyright © 2021 Liz Ashlee
All rights reserved.

ISBN: (ebook) 978-1-953335-61-6
(print) 978-1-953335-62-3

Inkspell Publishing
207 Moonglow Circle #101
Murrells Inlet, SC 29576

Cover art By Fantasia Frog Designs

OTHER BOOKS BY LIZ ASHLEE

Step Toward You

Heart's a Mess

Sort of Normal

LIZ ASHLEE

DEDICATION

For my role model, best friend, and mom, Geoia Gauck, who helped me brainstorm this idea while we were grocery shopping—and who's talked me down many of times when I've felt exactly like Hope does. Love you to the moon and back, Meme.

LIZ ASHLEE

WISHING ON WATER

Facebook isn't for the faint of heart. Neither is Twitter, Instagram, or any other type of social media. In fact, the whole idea of being *social* is a stab-in-the-back waiting to happen.

They're a reminder that life is happening all around me, while mine stagnates.

Boring.

I'm a creature of habit—I *like* boring. I like how I can count on eating dinner with my parents and brother every night, being in bed by nine to enjoy some reading, and sleeping in on the weekends. Between school and my part-time job, my hopes and dreams center on pure laziness. Eventually when I graduate college, I'll have a degree in math but also one in how-to-be-a-bum.

Everyone I've ever possibly known is doing things—*life* things.

Having babies.

Getting engaged or married.

Buying houses, new cars, couches, animals.

I might as well be a meme people share when their "single" status has been the same for so long it's dusty.

Just today five of my friends announced their

engagement. I have about five-hundred friends, which means if five people got engaged every day, it would take only a hundred days for everyone on my social network to find another person to love forever, while I worry about keeping my fish alive.

Somehow, forever alone feels more fitting as eternally alone, because even in death I'll be dancing with singlehood.

"Hope," my mom says, knocking on my doorframe. "Are you wasting away in self-pity again?"

I throw my hand over my face and drop my phone to my side. "Why do I do this to myself?"

She sits on my bed. I already feel one of those your-time-will-come speeches coming on. She'll say how I'm only twenty and have a lifetime ahead of me. True, but it seems bleak when literally everyone you know already has a life.

"Because you're off from school and you have nothing else to think about," she tells me gently.

Her words only make me feel worse. "Great, now I sound more pathetic."

"You're not pathetic, sweetie. You're just on a different path."

I squeeze my eyes closed beneath my hand. "A different path," I repeat.

"Yes," she says. "One where your life starts when you least expect it."

She tucks my hair behind my ear. I inherited the red color from my dad. My mom always tells me she's jealous of it, but I've always wished I could have the blonde hair her and my brother, Sam, have. Not that I don't like my hair color, just how along with it, I also inherited my dad's freckles, pale skin, and fear of the sun. "Don't be so down on yourself. Your big moments are coming. I promise."

I smile. "I'll hold you to it."

"You should," she agrees. The doorbell rings downstairs and my mom's face scrunches up. "I should

2

answer it because Sam won't. We really need to get him into a twelve-step program for gaming." She stands and points at my phone. "Speaking of which, how about you put that thing away?"

"I should, shouldn't I?" When she leaves, I do. I silence it and put it face down on my desk. My angst is only the summer blues. I feel lost without school. Eventually things will straighten out. I won't be panicking over babies, marriages and real social media things. Even if it doesn't feel like it, my life is on track. Mom's right—I'm just on a different time line.

"Hope? It's Chloe!" she yells.

In all of my moping and self-pity, I don't remember any texts from my best friend asking if she could come over. We're not spur of the moment people. It's why we gravitated toward each other in the first place, over a mutual fear of substitute teachers back when we were in elementary school.

My worrying, type-A friend doesn't just show up. I walk into the hall then down the stairs. Chloe's standing at the bottom with a huge grin on her face. She's wearing a blue dress, which is much nicer than my tank top and ratty shorts. Even her brown hair is out of its usual braid and is straightened. She *doesn't* look like she's had a boring day.

Before my foot hits the bottom step, she holds up her hand. Right there, on her ring finger, is a gold band with a sparkling diamond. My heart somehow defies modern medicine as it flutters with excitement for her and plummets to the ground.

"You're engaged?" I ask, trying to pretend my squeal is out of excitement.

My mom's face pops out of the living room. She probably knows exactly what I'm thinking.

Chloe nods happily. "As of this morning!"

"What? How?" *Why?*

Don't get me wrong, I'm beyond excited for her. She's been dating her boyfriend, Andrew, for a year now. When they got together, she gave me an inkling of hope I could find someone, too. Like me, she'd been dancing miserably with single-hood for a while, but then the Significant Other Gods decided it was her turn.

It's hard to think of her as being ahead of me. We've always been neck and neck when it comes to life. Same grades, same personality, same obsessions, same life goals. We even had our first periods within a week of each other. But now, she's getting married—starting a life.

And I'm...exactly where I've always been. *What's wrong with me?*

"This morning, Andrew took me to the park—the one we met in. He had a picnic set up and we went for a walk. He proposed to me on the bridge near the pond!" She continues to chatter excitedly about the details of the proposal and I fight to listen. All I can hear is the ticking of the clock on our living room mantle.

I'm only twenty. I have a *whole* life ahead of me. Maybe I'll be one of those people who wait until they're thirty to settle down. I mean, a Buzzfeed quiz I took last week said that I'd get married between the ages of twenty-six and thirty-two.

"So, what do you say?" Chloe finishes.

I blink.

"I say...okay?" I answer, hoping for the best.

She starts jumping again. "Thank goodness. I know should've done something cute to ask you to be my MOH, but we're not really like that."

My heart stammers. Maybe we're not quite as alike as I thought, because I have a whole Pinterest page dedicated to asking her to be my maid of honor, just like I do for the rest of my someday, maybe wedding.

Then again, that could be what's gotten me here. Some people are doers and others are planners. I'm a planner, not a doer. I make lists and Pinterest pages, but nothing comes of it. They don't do anything other than make me sad.

#

Chloe leaves an hour later, still over the moon. I managed to put on an excited face. I felt genuine happiness for her. Andrew's a good guy and they belong together—it's not their fault I'm in the mood to feel sorry for myself.

We glossed over some of her ideas for the wedding before she had to leave for a celebratory lunch with Andrew and her family.

The second she'd left, it felt as if she took all of the excitement with her. Now I'm hallow and sad. *Lonely.*

Mom's clearly trying to cure me because she's treating me like I'm defective. She's given me a mug of hot tea, despite it being warm out, and some chocolate chip cookies. She even drug Sam down to sit with us, although he's got his headphones in while he plays on his cell. I'm half-surprised she didn't order my dad to come home from work.

"Mom, I'm fine," I lie.

She rolls her eyes and sits down to the side of me, across from Sam. "No, you're not. Usually you're happy, a little snarky, but overall a good kid. Right now, you look like your fish died."

"Thank God, he didn't. He's all I have."

"*And* you're being dramatic."

"Sorry," I say. "I don't like being a drama queen."

"It's okay," she says. "What would make you feel better?"

I think about her question as I nibble on my cookies. When they're all gone, I take a sip of the tea to give myself some more reflection time. All the while, Sam plays his game. He's a senior in high school, but I wonder if he has the same fears as I do. Maybe he doesn't—maybe guys are wired differently. Then again, this might just be me. I think that's my biggest fear.

"I want to be different," I answer slowly. "I want to do something."

"Alright," she says. "That's a start."

I bite my lip. "I want to find myself."

"Like in the hippie sense?"

"Yeah, I think so. Is that weird?"

"Not if it would make you happy."

"I'm not sure how to do it, though. I feel so...it's like I don't change. My life stays the same. I do the same things, live in the same place. I just want something different." I wrap my fingers around the handle of my mug. "I want to get away from everything and start fresh."

She stares at me. I'm not sure if it's because she had me young, but she's always treated me like I'm an adult. The older I get, the more she feels like a friend and less like a mom. We've reached this stage where she's no longer raising me, she's helping me raise myself. She's not quite there with Sam yet, since I somehow matured in dog years and he still hasn't gotten out of his puppy phase.

"Okay."

"I said the same to Chloe when I had no idea what she said," I point out. "Which I feel really guilty about."

"No, I heard you. I'm thinking."

She stands and goes into the kitchen. She starts rifling through our pile of old mail, looking a little frazzled. When she finds what she's searching for, she holds it up and does a little dance.

"What's that?"

"A letter from your great-aunt Isla."

"No, I meant the dance."

She waves me off and walks back to her chair. She sits down and puts the letter on the table, then taps it. "This is your solution. Every year she offers for us to come stay with her and we always turn her down, because there's not enough room for all of us. But you? One person? Hope, you should go stay with her. Enjoy a summer on a beach, away from here, and away from social media."

"Seriously?"

"As serious as serious can be," she says. "I'll even pay for the plane ticket."

"Great-Aunt Isla lives in a retirement community—" I stop my complaint and reconsider. Which, now that I think about it, wouldn't be such a bad deal. Most of them aren't getting married, they're definitely not having babies, and they're in their forever homes. Their lives are figured out already. They've *been* figured out. If I'm lucky, it might even rub off on me. "Are you sure it's okay?"

"I'll call and ask, but I'm sure it is."

"What about work?" I ask. I'm a little interested to see how she'll explain away this one.

"Well, I don't usually support letting somebody down, but they're constantly calling you in on your days off and your manager loves you. I say you just reap what you're owed."

Well played, Mom. I draw in a deep breath, then let it out with a shaky smile. "Am I really going to do this?"

#

I'm actually doing this.

Strangely, it didn't sink in when I asked my manager if I could take two weeks off (or when she said yes and told me I deserve the time off, even though all I do is take coffee orders). It also didn't sink in when I kissed my parents and Sam goodbye at the airport or when I was sitting on the plane, traveling alone for the first time in my life.

Nope, it finally hits when my cab drops me off in front of an expansive three-story building which looks more like a high-end hotel than a place for the elderly. Not that I really know what a retirement home looks like. But if this is how they all are, I'm cashing in my student ID for an AARP card.

The only issue is I don't think I could afford the rent

Aunt Isla pays.

She's my maternal grandma's sister and probably the coolest person I know. Instead of getting married and starting a family, she traveled around the world, visiting at least seventy countries. Her passport is a colorful collage of a life well lived. It led her to starting a popular travel company. Before she retired, she'd made good investments which would've easily made the second half of her life livable, but she also sold the company for more zeros than I've ever seen. No one in my family knows the exact amount of money in her bank account, but I don't think we'd be able to comprehend it if we did.

Spending a few weeks with her might be good for me. I think I have a narrowed vision of how my life should be and Aunt Isla has an expansive view. She lives a life completely outside of the box and outside expectations—most importantly, she's happy.

I wheel my suitcase behind me as I walk up the roundabout and into the building. There's a sitting area to my left and an "information" desk to my right. There's a set of doors straight ahead, but you clearly can't just walk through them without permission. I turn to the desk and am met with a smiling middle-aged woman dressed in blue scrubs.

"Hello," she says.

"Hi." I stand my suitcase on end then walk up to the desk. "I'm Hope, and I'm here to stay with my Aunt Isla."

The woman claps. "Oh, yes. You have no idea how excited she is to have you stay with her. It's all she's been talking about."

"I'm excited, too," I say, taken a bit aback. I was worried she didn't really *want* me to visit as much as she felt it was kind to offer.

"Let me give her a quick call." She uses a phone on her desk and has a quick conversation telling my aunt I'm here. "Isla will be right down," she says after she hangs up.

"Thank you," I say and go wait in the common area.

Eventually, the door opens and Aunt Isla walks through. She's trendier than ever, in a large olive-colored poncho and a pair of black pants. She has on an array of clunky bracelets and necklaces, with earrings to match. Her short red hair—not natural like mine—is exceptionally cute and styled. She's the type of woman we all aspire to be when we get older. Also, one who gives Helen Mirren a run for her money.

"Hope!" she says cheerily as she comes toward me, arms open. She hugs me tightly. The smell I always associate with her, fresh gardenias, infiltrates my senses. "I'm so happy you're here!" She pulls back and looks me over. "You're absolutely gorgeous!" She peeks over my shoulder. "Isn't she pretty, Mary?"

"She is, Isla," Mary answers. "I'll bet she'll turn a few heads around here."

I blush. I needed to hear that, because I tend to identify most with a class-A troll, which isn't pretty on the ego.

Aunt Isla ticks my nose. "If you flirt some, you might be able to get some inheritance out of someone."

"Are you allowed to say that?" I ask, laughing.

She waves me off. "I can say anything I want. It's a benefit of being old. Anyway, it might not be worth it considering you have mine to look forward to. But let's not think about that! So morbid."

She takes my hand in hers and gives me the chance to grab my suitcase, before she drags me away. The door clicks and opens, letting us inside. She leads me down a hallway, then stops at a door halfway down. Her name is written on it in neat, cursive handwriting.

"I apologize ahead of time you'll be sleeping on the couch. At least it pulls out," she says.

"I'll be fine," I promise her. If I know Aunt Isla, she probably didn't go cheap on her pull out couch. It's probably more comfortable than my bed. I have a feeling, if not for my parents (and maybe Sam), I'd *never* want to leave here.

Her apartment matches her personality with its eclectic decor. It's spacious, which isn't what I expected—I guess I pictured something similar to a motel. Instead, there's a full sized kitchen and living room, which are bigger than my entire house. Nothing really matches in either room, but it all somehow goes together. My favorite part of the entire place is her curio cabinet. Inside, she stores an elephant for every different place she's visited. Each one is unique and gorgeous. She'd even sent me a matching one after her Paris trip because I asked. It has little golden Eiffel Towers etched into the saddle. It's my most prized possession.

"I know you probably want to get settled in, but how about in an hour, we go meet some people? Did you bring your swimsuit?"

#

Aunt Isla has more energy than a person half her age. I feel tired just watching her. She buzzed around her apartment, chitchatting about everything, until I finally told her I was ready to leave. I didn't find it annoying—I loved it. My mom's a lot like her and I hope I'm like my mom.

I change into my two-piece bathing suit, which might as well be a one-piece. Aunt Isla lets me borrow one of her cover-ups, and wears one herself. Her bathing suit reminds me of something from the forties. She also gives me a large lipped hat to wear. Somehow it all makes me feel glamorous.

"My friends are going to *love* you," she says as we travel the hallways to the swimming area behind the building. The beach isn't far beyond, but Aunt Isla said they only go there on special occasions. "We might drown," she explains. "Evidently we're old, so we need a lifeguard."

"I don't think old has anything to do with it," I tell her jokingly. "*I* would need a lifeguard, too."

"I guess following the rules means you can sue them if

you drown."

"Nobody can sue anyone if they're dead," I point out, making her grin.

"You have the best humor," she says. "I'm going to claim it's because of my genes."

I'm sure she's right. My dad has a drier sense of humor, which can be super hilarious, but you have to listen carefully to catch it. So, obviously it comes from my mom's side.

We're met with laughter and loud voices when we step outside. It seems as if everyone is back here, either in the pool or by it. Clearly they have their own cliques because they're all bunched together in groups.

Aunt Isla leads us over to one of the poolside tables, where there are two empty seats. Three people are already there. One is an African American man wearing a Hawaiian shirt and swim trunks, along with a dapper, tan hat. Another is a woman who looks younger than the others and is flaunting it—wearing a bikini top and a high-waisted skirt. The final woman has long gray hair and is wearing a peasant shirt. Her eyes are glassy and there's a vacant look on her face.

"This is Hope," Aunt Isla tells them. "Hope, this is Arthur, my special friend." I choke. *Special friend?* What does that even mean? I'm not sure I want to know. "Shirley, the floozy. And Marilyn, the sweet but forgetful one."

I wave, which earns me a wave back from Arthur, a side-eye from Shirley, and a huge grin from Marilyn. Aunt Isla sits down next to Arthur and taps the other vacant seat. I take it. There's no missing how Arthur immediately twines his hand with hers. How did we not know about him?

"So, how're you liking it here so far?" Arthur asks.

"The place is beautiful." I'm not sure if I'm really liking the trip, per say. I love Aunt Isla and getting to see her is a dream. The only problem comes with seeing Aunt Isla and

Arthur together. It's clear love exists in old age, too. There's no escaping it. At least, there will be no babies, new home, or life changes to worry about.

I hope.

Here I am blaming social media for all my troubles, but maybe it's all on me.

"It had better be," Shirley says. "My children pay a pretty penny to hide me away in here. Only the best for a mom they don't want to see." She crooks her finger at me to lean in and lowers her voice. "Life lesson: your children will hold resentment toward you if you're married four times. You love them and raise them, then next thing you know, they're telling a therapist about how you ruined them."

"Hogwash," Aunt Isla interrupts. "Your children love you."

"I never said they didn't," Shirley replies.

Aunt Isla rolls her eyes, but smiles. "Let's not scare the girl off. You don't want *her* talking to a therapist about you, too."

Arthur shakes his head at the two of them, then looks at me. "You'll learn these two'll wear you out. It's almost like they feed off each other." He gives a look at his watch. "You have ten more minutes till you're free to breathe."

"More like ten minutes until we die," Aunt Isla says dramatically.

"What's in ten minutes?" Marilyn asks, piping up. She has a strong draw to her voice, as if she should be drinking sweet tea on the veranda.

"Water aerobics, dear," Shirley says, patting her on the arm.

"You can watch or mill around," Aunt Isla tells me. "Or you can swim. I would not do the aerobics, mind you. They're god-awful."

"I guess I should go get my swimsuit on," Marilyn says, starting to stand.

"Sweetie," Shirley says, gently. "You already have it

on."

"Oh," Marilyn whispers, blushing.

"What's wrong?" Shirley asks her. She gives me a sly wink, which Marilyn misses. "*You* reminded *me* to slip mine on in the first place, Mar."

"I did?" Marilyn asks.

"You did," Arthur confirms. He automatically receives points for his kindness.

"Speaking of reminders, somebody please remind me *Paul's* stopping by to fix my faucet. I need to look my best," Shirley tells us all, then starts adjusting her bathing suit top.

"Every woman—other than me, Arthur—and some men are vying for Paul's heart," Aunt Isla says. "What makes you think you'll be special?"

Does she mean "special" in the same way she called Arthur her "special friend?" "Who's Paul?" I ask.

"He's our resident dreamboat," Aunt Isla tells me. "He's leading man material. Like Cary Grant."

"*Better* than Cary Grant," Shirley clarifies.

It makes me smile they're sitting around talking about cute guys. At least, some things never change, whether you're a teenager or you're in your retirement. I honestly can't wait to see this Paul to know what they find "dreamy."

"And he's deaf in one ear—wounded from the army. It's so sweet," Shirley says, fanning herself.

"Half of us are deaf around here," Arthur points out. "And half of us served in the war."

"And we're grateful for that, love," Aunt Isla says. "It's okay to be jealous."

"I'm not jealous," he mutters, almost pouting.

A beeping starts, interrupting their banter, and they all stand. "That's our cue," Aunt Isla tells me. "I'll be done in an hour and a half."

I decide to take my chances and visit the ocean. Barely a day into the trip and I've developed a devil-may-care attitude, tempting death by going lifeguard-less

I sit so the water just barely touches my toes. My mom used to tell me if you wished on water, your wish would travel across the world so it could come true. The idea made me so giddy, thinking how easy it sounded. I once wished for Sam to get into a summer-long camp for science. I visualized my wish traveling through streams and drains to the committee members' houses.

When the water drifts all the way up to my heels, I close my eyes and let out a breath. *I wish this summer would help me find what I'm missing.*

#

The next day we take a bus into town. The bus does a town-and-back trip everyday so the residents have the chance to go out and run their errands since all the stores are centrally located. There's a definite seating arrangement, sorted by cliques. Shirley, Marilyn, Arthur, Aunt Isla, and I took the open seats near the emergency exit. Shirley told me matter-of-factly, they always take those seats because there's more room for their purchases. I'm sure about two things: (1) it's not safe to pile groceries in front of the emergency exit and (2) these four rule the roost around here.

Arthur wasn't planning on going out today, but tagged along anyway. He and Aunt Isla must spend virtually all of their time together, despite living separately. The love between them is palpable and I hope I'll somehow absorb it just by being near them. When Aunt Isla sat beside me on the bus, she immediately reached for his hand between the seats. Then once we came to a stop, Arthur helped her up. Theirs is a quiet love, but that only makes it more beautiful.

"*We* have a salon date," Shirley says, one arm linked through Marilyn's as she fluffs her hair with her free hand.

"Please tell me it's not for Paul," Arthur groans.

"No, we're going to see Marilyn's handsome doctor tomorrow," Shirley says coyly, as they part from us and start across the street.

"In case you didn't know it, Shirley is Marilyn's sister-in-law. She takes real nice care of her in memory of her older brother," Arthur explains to me as we walk into the grocery store.

"What's wrong with Marilyn?" I ask.

Arthur and I wait while Aunt Isla grabs a cart. He leans on his cane. "She has dementia. It was slow at first, but it's gotten worse. Shirley's worried Marilyn will have to go off to a different facility."

"Marilyn seems lonely," I observe, remembering how she'd talked about her kids.

He nods. "She has a family and a lot of money, but I'd say the only good thing she's really got is Shirley."

"And you and Aunt Isla."

"Yeah, and us," he says. He taps my foot with his cane, a mischievous twinkle in his eye. "Lucky her."

"Are you two bonding?" Aunt Isla asks, rolling her cart toward us.

"She already favors me over you," Arthur tells her.

"It's true," I agree.

Aunt Isla rolls her eyes and leads us further into the store. About halfway through her groceries, she asks me to head over to the dessert section and find us something sweet to eat tonight. I happily take her up on that because, well, sweets.

My attention is immediately drawn to the different flavors of fudge boxed up, calling to me like the gates of Fort Knox. The advertising claims it's local, handmade, and fresh, and if I want more there's a store. I pick one of them up, trying to smell it.

"You can't go wrong with that one, but I'd do cookie dough."

I jump, nearly dropping the box. *Crap.* Here I am sniffing this box like a fudge-head. If I wasn't a total and complete weirdo before, I am now. I mean, without turning around, I already know this guy's going to be attractive. It's in his voice. Deep, southern and rolling as the hills I just flew over. This, right here, is a reason why *forever alone* is my relationship status for life. I can't even do something alone (at least I thought I was alone) without embarrassing myself.

I set the box down—mint chocolate chip—and turn around. My ears were right in their assumption. He's more attractive than anyone I've ever seen. Not *hot* or *sexy*— terms I might normally use to describe the ideal man—but *handsome*. His hair is curly on top and as rich in color as dark chocolate, but shorter on the sides. Thick eyebrows sit atop soulful, brown eyes rimmed with thick lashes. His skin has such a deep tan it's almost as if the sun decided to just merge with him rather than burn him.

He blinds me with a dazzling, white grin. Holy fire-panties, he might have *ate* the sun with the wattage of his smile. There are even little lines in his cheeks which aren't quite dimples, but are somehow better.

"Sorry to catch you off guard," he says.

I blink. Thanks to the love-deprived woman I am today, I'm about as good at conversing with an attractive man as I am at talking to a brick wall. "Y-you're fine." I set the box back before I murder the fudge. *That* would be the only thing worse than what's happening right now. I take the rest of him in. He's wearing a pair of khakis and a black short sleeve shirt which shows a set of well-defined muscles that aren't too bulky or too lean. In one hand is a half-gallon of milk and in the other is a wrench which was possibly used to kill Ms. Peacock in the Kitchen. "Probably not a good idea to sneak up on someone with that," I say, stupidly. To make matters worse, I point at the milk.

He chuckles. Maybe I'm not as bad at this as I think I am. Maybe I'm funny.

Ish.

"Just be glad it wasn't the full gallon," he says and

winks. *Winks.* I've seen creepy people, actors and elders wink, but never anyone else. I always thought winking was one of those weird things people do to be cute, even though it really makes them look like they've got a twitch. This guy's definitely the exception. My stomach has fluttering wings and angry hippos barreling around—good, yet intense.

So *this* is how you're supposed to feel around the opposite sex. It's nothing compared to the minor feelings I've had about crushes, where my hands might shake or I might feel a little warm. Two seconds into meeting him and I'm pretty sure I'm in love.

Okay, so not "love," but maybe lust. That doesn't even sound right—affection? All I know is I can already hear wedding bells and feel rice falling on me.

I swear to goodness, if the next words out of my mouth are "I do," I'm either going to go into hibernation or join a convent. My mind is taking this a few years too far into the future.

His mouth starts to move, but I'm too busy watching him like he's some sort of work of art in an exhibit. Maybe a museum—see attractive man not known to woman-kind since the dawn of the twenty-first century and Internet.

He pauses and tilts his head, then drags me back to reality by clearing his throat.

I squint and tuck my hair behind my ear. My mom is always telling me I need to keep it out of my face and how if people can see my face, I automatically appear more confident, even when I'm lacking.

"Sorry, I was just..." I trail off. Tucking the hair didn't help at all. How would I even finish that? *Sorry, I was just checking you out and planning our life.* Ew. "What were you saying?"

His grin grows; clearly, he's enjoying this. There's something wolfish about his canine teeth. At least, it makes him less perfect, if not more adorable. "I was just saying you should definitely choose the chocolate-chip cookie dough."

"Really?"

"Well, I mean, I like mint, but it's overwhelming after a while," he explains, genuinely excited to tell me this fact.

"Sounds like a reason *to* choose mint," I say more to myself and my thighs. "No, I was asking what you were really saying?"

"Well, yeah, there's not much further you can take a joke about a milk jug. Sure, there might've been something less than cool thrown in there, but..." he shrugs it off. Great, so he gets to just shrug off his uncoolness, while I'm going to be haunted by mine thirty years from now when I'm *still* cringing over this. "Anyway, sorry again for scaring you."

He somehow manages to grab his own box of cookie dough fudge, even with the wrench and milk, expertly holding it between his arm and his side. His weight shifts as he moves to walk away. I can feel our moment slipping through my fingers. I don't know if being in a different state has me feeling extra confident (or, arguably, stupid), but I snatch my own box and say, "If you're wrong, I'm suing you."

He turns to face me with a wry smile, somehow completely different than his previous grin. Goodness, it's as if those lips speak their own language. "I'm never wrong."

"That's not probable." I'm trying to flirt, but I never learned how to. Instead, all I know is how to be awkward and talk in math-speak.

"But possible," he argues.

I can't hold back a smile. That's basically the *exact* answer I wanted. I think this means we're meant to be. "I hope for your money's sake, it's very possible."

He chuckles, swaying on the balls of his feet and tilting his head slightly. I catch a glimpse of faded scars running up from his shirt and toward his ear, reminding me of tree branches. Part of the shell of his ear is missing. It's weird

I'm just now noticing it. He doesn't hold himself like he'd be scarred so visibly. I can't help but respect him.

"So, are you a transplant or a vacationer?" he asks. He sets the milk down on the table, along with the box, settling in. He leans against the display and crosses his arms, still nonchalantly holding the wrench.

"What makes you think I'm one of those?"

He shrugs. "I'd have noticed you, if you weren't."

A fiery blush stampedes up my neck and over my cheeks. I'm sure it only makes my hair look extra bright. What does he mean, he'd have noticed me? I'm not really noticeable. I had one or two guys like me in high school, but they were friends first and were probably a result of falling for my personality, not perceiving my looks. I've felt invisible around other people—watching and witnessing, but never interacting.

Maybe he just means it's a small town and everyone knows everyone.

"I'm visiting my aunt for a few weeks," I explain. "You live here?"

The man seems to have an unlimited amount of smiles in his back pocket. "My whole life, with a few gap years somewhere else." Somehow his eyes darken and his mouth twitches slightly, as if there's something going unsaid he's uncomfortable about. He gathers himself just as quickly as he lost himself. "Guess you might always be right, too, huh?"

I hug my box tightly to my chest and take a small step toward him. We're a few feet apart in our little empty corner of the store. I hope it's not too noticeable I'm creeping on him. I just want to be closer. There's something about him pulling me in.

"I'm not as lucky as you are in that department," I admit.

"Ah," he says, eying me over.

"I'm only human," I continue.

"Not everyone can be as great as me," he says dryly. My

eyes widen, worried he's serious, then he starts to laugh at my reaction, so I do, too. "How long have you been in town?"

"Since yesterday."

He nods as if impressed. "And already needing the fudge."

"No, I'm having fun. This is just...dessert. My aunt suggested picking up something sweet."

"I'm joking with you," he says. "Fudge isn't something to drown your sorrows in, anyway."

I bite my lip. If I keep smiling at him, I'll look manic. I point at his wrench. "Are you going to cut the fudge with that?"

He laughs. "It's making you nervous, eh?"

"My parents aren't very handy," I tell him. "Tools mean disaster in my household. My dad once broke his toe with one of those."

"I can see the cause for concern, then." He taps it lightly against his forearm, which makes all the muscles in his arms dance beneath his perfectly tanned skin. "I lost my old one. Things tend to go missing where I work."

I wonder if he's in construction and that's what happened to his ear. It would make sense. "Convenience store to the rescue."

"Always. One of these days, this town will get a hardware store," he says. "That day will probably come when I'm long gone, though. This place just got rid of their phone booth a few years ago. They also still have gas pump attendants."

"I guess that's why a lot of older people gravitate here."

"Not a bad place to retire," he agrees.

An awkward silence settles between us. He doesn't make any move to leave our area and I stand there staring at my sandaled feet. I'm not sure how to start up a new conversation or how to end this. I really need to be getting back to Aunt Isla and Arthur, but I want to stay with this guy. He's funny and nice and I feel like I'm experiencing something I've always missed out on. *An opportunity.*

He clears his throat suddenly, and I look at him hopefully. He reaches into his pocket and pulls out a cell phone. "You're here for a few weeks, you said?"

I nod, but realize he can't see me because he's paying attention to his phone. "Yes."

He holds out his phone to me, giving me a sincere smile. "Then I'd like to see you again, if it's all right."

I take it from him and stare down at the new contact screen, while he waits for me to fill it with my information. Giddiness bubbles up inside my chest and insecurity pops it. I want this to be because he's interested in me, but it might also be because he wants me to have a friend in town.

No, I'm going to be hopeful. I'm going to take this chance, because friend or romantic interest, I like him enough to deal with either.

My fingers shake as I type in my name and number. I mess up a few times, even though my name is short, and have to start over. I don't trust myself to say anything to him until I've saved it and handed the phone back to him.

"I'd love that." My voice is barely above a whisper.

His brows draw close together, but quickly part, and looks from me down to my phone. "I'll text you later, Hope."

He grabs his things and walks off. No, not walks. *Saunters.* When he's gone, I wonder if he was ever really standing in front of me. I check my phone, but there's no evidence of him there, either. I could be so lovesick I imagined it all, thanks to too many romance-binges on Netflix and on my Kindle. Even if he does exist, there's always a chance he won't text me and I can't text him because I don't have his number.

Or his name.

#

There's something about Arthur that makes me think a lifetime of being single wouldn't be so bad if you had someone like him waiting for you near the end. I pluck up the courage to ask about their relationship after the groceries are put away and we've eaten some dinner, and are now munching on individual hearty-sized pieces of fudge.

Aunt Isla smiles around her mouthful, nodding to Arthur to tell me. "Well, I fell in love with Isla when I was—what—ten? She walked home from school by my house every day. Her hair was long and in pigtails. My dreams always had those braids woven in them." He reaches for her free hand and brings it up to his lips to kiss. "Times were different then, as we all know. So, I never got up the courage to talk to her."

Aunt Isla sets down her piece to continue. "My visit to China made it into the newspaper. I wanted to paint their scenery. It was my first trip overseas and I was excited and terrified. On the day I was leaving, there was a little package in our mailbox with my name on it. He'd carved an elephant out of wood and put my initials on it. He wrote a note, too."

"That's why you collect elephants." My heart flutters with emotion. "It's so sweet."

Arthur grins. "We wrote often—all our lives."

"But you never met face to face?" If they had, I'm sure things would have gone differently. "Did you ever start a family?"

"No and no," he replies. "I was waiting, I guess. Five years ago, I had a health scare—prostate cancer. I decided if I didn't have control over how long my life would be, I wanted to have control over what happens in it. So, I moved here to be near Isla."

"When he told me about his plans, he explained he only expected friendship from me. There was no way, after all these years, I wouldn't want more."

They squeeze each other's hand, gazes locked. I love

getting to witness this, as if I'm at the foundation of true love. It's a reminder it always exists, even if you have to wait for it.

"But your health—are you better now?" I ask.

Arthur lets go of Aunt Isla's hand and points at me. "Now, don't go worrying about me. I'm fine. They say you'll get another cancer before prostate cancer kills you. It's slow progressing." He pops the last of his fudge into his mouth with a crooked grin. "You girls are stuck with me for a time to come."

"Lucky us," Aunt Isla says, crinkling her nose. Someone knocks on the door and she stares at it blankly. "Who's that?"

Arthur's smile melts away. "Paul. My competition."

Aunt Isla laughs. "With all the excitement over Hope, I completely forgot I asked Paul to stop by to look at my TV." She claps her hands together excitedly. If I didn't know any better, I'd almost think there's a conspiratorial tint to her eyes. "Oh, I can't wait for you to meet Paul, Hope. He's such a sweetheart."

"And a dreamboat," I add.

"The man has more girlfriends around here than you can count and you'll see why," she says, walking toward the door. "Coming!"

I spin in my chair, resting my arms on the back of it. I don't know why I'm so excited to meet this Paul. He's a looking glass into what a gorgeous guy looks like in the eyes of a retiree. Evidently he's deaf, but a veteran, and he must be handy—but is he only attractive because he's handy? My mom used to say there's nothing more attractive than a man who is willing to work without issue. Then again, maybe he's like Harrison Ford and manages to stay young because of a certain rugged handsomeness and a lot of personality.

Only the door opens up and I'm wrong about it all.

About fifty years wrong.

"You're the dreamboat?" I blurt out.

I immediately throw my hand over my mouth, feeling like a fool. I feel duped! I swear they've been leading me to believe Paul's an older gentleman, but really he's a strapping twenty-something with eyes darker than oil and a smile that silently speaks a thousand languages.

Somehow *their* Paul also happens to be *my* grocery-store guy. In any other situation, this would be the perfect meet cute. Some beautiful fate decided to bestow me not one, but two, chance meetings with him. Fate's got nothing against me when my voice's censor goes out, leaving Paul just as stunned as I feel.

Isla waves at me from behind him, then makes a shushing motion. Beside me, Arthur rolls his eyes. "Shouldn't have said that, Hope. It's the worst kept secret around these parts, but the women like to believe he doesn't know it."

Mr. Circa-1990's Model scratches at his chin with his free hand. The other hand is holding a toolbox with, you guessed it, a wrench slung through the handle. "And, I act like I don't," he agrees. He's not cocky about what these women think, thankfully.

I swallow. Fight or flight bubbles up inside me and I want to choose *flight* and head straight for the next plane home, where I can then spend the rest of eternity hiding out beneath my blankets. Too bad my legs won't move. I feel like I'm stuck in a mob-centric cement encasing, with only my face to use. It would explain my diarrhea of the mouth and why my cheeks are so hot they're boiling.

"Sorry. I didn't mean to..." I trail off. I didn't mean to do anything, because I haven't had the time to think anything through. I just sort of blurted it out. "I hope I didn't embarrass you. Not that I'm taking back the dreamboat part, because you...well. I just shouldn't have said it out loud." I offer him a shaky smile. "I was led to think an older gentleman who looked like Cary Grant was going to walk through the door."

"How were you led to believe *that*?" Aunt Isla asks with

a laugh. "We never said his age."

I shrug, unable to meet anyone's eyes. "I guess it was more of an assumption."

Aunt Isla clucks her tongue. I can feel her giving me a look of sympathy, scorching me worse than the sun did today. "Arthur, would you mind helping Paul?" Arthur gives her a strange look and rolls his eyes. He doesn't say a word as he walks over to the TV and stands there, waiting.

I glance up and find Paul staring at me, his head tilted. I had previously thought Aunt Isla's apartment was large, but now it feels small with his tall, muscular body filling the space. It's like all of the air is being taken up. When he smiles, I sneak in the last breath I think I'll ever breathe. "Dreamboat," he mouths, then grins and walks toward Arthur.

Aunt Isla faces me and leans in. "*That's* how you speak to a young, single, handsome young man?" she whispers.

I reach up to fluff my messy bun, needing to do something with all of my nervous energy. "Evidently. I don't have a lot of practice."

"I can tell," she agrees.

"I was surprised and he's well...he made me nervous, okay?" I say, pulling my lip between my teeth. "He's cute. *Really* cute. And I'm weird. There's a reason why I'm single and we just witnessed said reason." I close my eyes and let out a sigh. It's loud and impossible not to hear, which makes me cringe. When I speak again, I drop my voice extra low. "I can't believe I said he was a dreamboat. *Twice.*"

She reaches out and pats my arm reassuringly. "Nobody's good at this sort of thing. I guess I just hoped it would go better."

"*Hoped?*" The word is at full volume. I link my hand in hers and pull her in the direction of her bedroom. This conversation requires privacy. She shuts the door behind her and motions for me to sit down on her canopy bed. The room is all lace and quilted fabrics, with accents of purple and a pale green. It somehow feels exotic, yet homey and delicate. "What do you mean hoped?"

She shrugs, this time acting like the one who's said too much. "I won't lie. I sort of hoped you might get along with him."

"Did you break your TV on purpose?"

"I unplugged something. We old people do it all the time, you know. Some of us just need help plugging it back in, either because we don't know what we did or we just want to call Paul. So I did, seeing as I happen to have a very pretty, smart, and interesting grand-niece who I think he might be good with."

Interesting usually is a euphemism for weird. The only thing interesting about me is I got a perfect score on math ACT. Beyond that, I'm a certifiable nerd who prefers keeping social interactions to a minimum (for obvious reasons) and going to bed early (wearing fuzzy socks).

"I wish you would have told me."

"What do you think I was doing? The girls and I brought him up multiple times."

"I thought you were gossiping. And I thought he was—"

"Old?"

I nod. "Sorry."

"I guess it does go along with where we're at." She blows out an exasperated breath. "This wasn't my finest plan. Normally, I'm better at playing matchmaker. Actually, I've always been wonderful for everyone but myself. Maybe it's because I have Arthur now. He's throwing me off."

"It's me, don't blame Arthur."

She shakes her head. "And Paul. I expected better from him, too. I've never seen him look like a deer caught in the headlights before. Around women my age he's a flirt, but around you he might as well have been catatonic."

"Maybe he's into older women?" I offer. I would love to know what her version of flirting is, because the smile he gave me sure felt like flirting turned up to eleven. Unless I'm reading it wrong and he was just smiling at my expense...*stop, Hope.* I won't let myself think that way. He *was* looking at me like he liked me and he asked me for my number. I'm not going to keep ruining my self-confidence.

"No, trust me. He's not. He's been here since he was a baby—we all treat him as our own. That would be incest."

"But you all still flirt with him."

She waves at me. "Not the point."

I look at her door, wishing I could see through it. I doubt Paul and Arthur are having this conversation, considering Arthur is a little green-eyed when it comes to Paul. "What do I do now?"

"Well, you take Arthur's place helping while Arthur and I go visit Marilyn or something."

"What?"

Before I can argue, she's up and enacting phase two of her crazy plan. I follow behind her into the main room, where she grabs Arthur by the hand and pulls him away, whispering loudly, "Let's let Hope help Paul."

I stare at the door, even after it's shut and they're gone. I want to roll my eyes so far back into my head they get stuck, but I also have an even bigger urge to run outside and put my opposable thumbs to use hitchhiking. I'm stuck at a crossroad between being humored and terrified of the situation. Then there's also this stupid third urge, one that's barely visible and might be a little, *teenie* bit happy Aunt Isla's gone and done this. Evidently I can't find anyone on my own, so her playing matchmaker might be what I need. I just won't admit it out loud. *Ever.*

"I smell a set up," Paul says, jolting me out of my thoughts.

My gaze settles on him, bent over the back of the TV as he wrestles around with the cables. The man is as perfect from the back as he is the front. His shirt raises, revealing a sliver of his back and a tattoo which covers most of the exposed skin. Now I'm envisioning what his whole back looks like. The gray band of his boxers peeks out from his shorts. I *totally* get why the women around here like him so much—and evidently some of the men. He's definite man-candy.

We're given this clashing idea of what repair men look like—one the porno one and the other of the guy with the butt crack and the muffin top. Mr. Muffin is the one you get when you're younger, but Paul's type is reserved for later. He's some sort of a gift for older people.

"I'm sorry." I make my way toward him. "This is embarrassing."

"Yeah," he agrees. He stops what he's doing and turns toward me. I draw in a breath, my heartbeat suddenly turns frantic and heavy. A one-time meeting in a grocery store did not make me immune to his looks—if anything, it made me more affected by him. Now, I can see beyond the surface and see the small details. There's a small dimple in his left cheek, making his smile seem extra genuine. Or how his eyes have caramel flecks in them, glinting and glowing with the light of his grin. "But you learn to brush off what they say around here real quick."

I give him a wary look. "I hope the same goes for me?"

"I think what you said is going to stick with me for a real long time," he says, chuckling. He reaches up to scratch his chin, where there's the lightest of a five o'clock shadow brewing. "My ego grew about five sizes, thanks to you."

"My thinking you were old should knock you back down. All the facts added up to it."

"That's how *you* think they added up," he corrects.

"Really, though. I didn't know what my aunt was planning. You don't have to humor her if you don't want to."

He swallows, not looking at me. "What if I do, though?"

I blink. *What?* Before I can ask for more, he focuses back on the cables. "My aunt said she unplugged something on purpose," I tell him. "I don't want you to have to play Sherlock if there's no problem."

He chuckles. "They do that a lot around here. Sometimes on purpose, sometimes not."

"Because they want to look at you?" I ask. Once again, I'm immediately embarrassed by my dang words. .

"Yeah and I think they get lonely." He glances over his shoulder, giving me a smart-ass look. "Probably seventy-five percent your answer, twenty-five mine."

"At least, you're honest," I say.

He turns back to the television and begins looking for whatever is unplugged. I walk to the other side of the TV and look down at what he's doing. We both glance up at each other and my whole body turns into a mess of goo and tingles.

"This is dangerous work here," he says, raising his brow in irony.

"I think I'll survive." My voice sounds quieter than normal and a little country, as if I'm matching his accent. I can feel myself drifting toward him—not just my body, but everything inside of me. Heart, soul, mind. I break free of our staring contest first and look down at the plugs. "Oh!" I reach for the one out of its socket and plug it back in. I straighten and clap my hand over my chest. "I'm not sure how I survived it. Talk about quick sand."

"I've seen soldiers cry at a loose plug," Paul says, straightening, too. "You're some sort of super hero."

I blush, even though we're totally being sarcastic. "There's definitely a reason why you have a harem of elders," I admit.

He rolls his eyes. "They all either want to pinch my cheek or my ass—it's like they can't make up their mind."

He goes back to his toolbox and picks it up. I motion to the wrench. "So, what's the story behind the stolen tools?"

"Sometimes the residents think they can make repairs on their own, even though it's technically, not their property to fix. So, they take my things without me knowing and most of the time they forget they took it. Usually I have a guess as to who the culprit was, but it's no skin off my back to buy a new tool."

The way he talks causes his "aww" factor to raise. There's something sweet about him letting the residences have their independence, even though I'm sure it costs him time and money. As much as he jokes about the people here, he clearly loves them.

His weight shifts as he stuffs a hand into the pocket of his shorts. He looks like something out of a magazine. "I have to go repair a sink, but would you want to get out of here when I'm finished?"

I blink. Is he asking me out? I'm not sure if it's possible, but I stutter out a nod.

"I'll text you when I'm done," he says.

I stare at the door long after he's gone then let out an embarrassing shriek which I'm glad no one's around to hear. "I'm going on a date!"

My fist pumps and victory rounds immediately end when I realize *I'm going on a date.*

By the time Aunt Isla makes it back to me—Arthur-less—I'm somewhere between floating on cloud nine and hyperventilating. I haven't been on a date since I was a high school senior two years ago which doesn't really mean anything considering all of my former dates were horrible. I'd honestly rather say I've never been on a date than admit what occurred on them.

The one where I thought the guy was into me, but only wanted to talk about Chloe.

The one where the guy shut the car door on my hand and broke my finger.

The one where I was set up with a guy who I was told was my age, but was creepily younger.

Rather than sitting at zero in terms of dating, I'm in the negatives. It doesn't matter how outgoing and handsome Paul is, or how dreamy the beach, or how Aunt Isla dresses me—I'm going to be a flustered, inexperienced dud.

How's that for self-confidence? Yeah, screw self-confidence. I'm pretty sure it's officially time to punch in my socially-awkward-and-self-deprecating card.

I'm in such a fog of fear, I somehow sleepwalk through Aunt Isla dressing me, then doing my hair and makeup. When she claps her hands, I jolt.

"Aren't you gorgeous, Hope?" she says.

I force myself out my daze to try to see what she's seeing. She curled my red hair so the waves in it are more natural and even, rather than a tangled, misshapen mess. By adding a layer of foundation to my face, my natural paleness glows. She even managed to find a lipstick shade which looks good on me—something I've always struggled to do. With her magical make-up talents, she makes my dull, brownish-greenish eyes stand out. My aunt must be some kind of witch with skills like these. Or she forgot to share about her years working at the Sephora counter.

She surprised me by getting giddy over an outfit I actually really like—a black buttoned-down dress which is formed fitting with a thicker material so not show any lumps or bumps. After buckling me a in a brown belt, she finished my ensemble with the tallest sandals I own.

"Wow..." I say in awe. I run my fingers through my hair, which feels softer and more voluminous than ever. I almost can't believe I'm the girl looking back at me, but I somehow feel more confident than ever. Maybe I need to start giving myself more credit. "You're a sorceress."

"Sweetie, I'm no such thing. This is all you—you were perfect pre-makeup and clothes. I think you just needed to see it."

My mom says similar things all the time, but it feels better hearing it from somebody who doesn't have to say it. "Thank you."

"We both know dressed up or not, Paul thinks you're pretty."

I blush. I hope to goodness she's right. "Do you think he'll be dressed this way, too? What if this isn't that sort of—"

She shushes me. "Paul's a gentleman, so I'm sure he'll look just as nice. And if he doesn't, I will take him to his apartment and dress him myself, whether he's in his mid-twenties or not."

I have no doubt she would, either. There's a knock at her door and my heartbeat accelerates to rabbit-speed. He texted me when we were finishing up my hair to say he would be here in about ten minutes.

I check the clock on the mantle—he's on time. It's like he's somehow ticking off all of my boxes.

I follow Aunt Isla to the front door, ankles and legs shaking. I shouldn't be nervous. I already know he's nice, cute and he likes me, too. It should make me feel calm and ready to embrace the moment. I'm about a million miles away from either of those.

When she opens the door, Paul stands on the other side holding a makeshift bouquet of flowers which I'm pretty sure came from the front lawn. He's wearing a pair of khakis again, only these are more formal looking. He also has on a blue button down shirt, with the sleeves rolled up to just below his elbows. *This* is somehow better than I'd hoped he'd look. In between the last time I saw him and now, he went from dream*boat* to dream-*yacht*.

He holds the flowers out to Aunt Isla, giving us both a sheepish grin as he rubs at the back of his neck with his free hand. "These are for both of you. I figured I take care of the grounds, so..." He trails off as she takes them and smells them. "Let's just keep it between us."

"As long as you're defacing the property for my niece, I suppose it's fine," Aunt Isla agrees, looking as if she's been bitten by the love bug herself. "Well, you two have fun." Paul steps out into the hallway, but she stops as me as I pass. "Do *everything* I would do," she whispers into my ear. "Find yourself a little, darling."

I'm speechless as she shuts the door. Did she just tell me to...yep, she definitely did. It's a good thing there's a layer of makeup on my face, or my blush could guide the ships to the shore.

Paul waves at a few of the other residents as we walk down to the main lobby. The woman behind the desk, different from the woman who I first met, eyes Paul longingly, but he just nods at her as we pass. He leads me to a tan Jeep, which has the zip in and out windows.

He follows me and goes to open my door just as I do. Our hands collide in what isn't exactly a romantic moment as much as it is a painful one. When I wince, he reaches for my hand and twines it with his, running his thumb over my injury.

The pain immediately dissipates and a numbness takes up the space instead. Not from our little accident, but from the way his rough, calloused skin feels against mine, which look like a child's compared to his. The sudden connection transfixes me. I'm amazed how contact so minor can make entire body feel as if it's been lit on fire. This isn't electricity, like I've heard talked about with romance, but closer to a burning which infiltrates every layer of my body. Electricity is fleeting, but this feels infinite—an immortal flame.

My breath hitches when I catch him watching me with an intense expression. Is this what they mean by a smoldering gaze? "Not used to a gentleman?" he asks.

"Not used to a man," I answer breathlessly before I can stop myself. My eyes go wide, but I can't steal my gaze away from his. "I don't know why I keep letting my mouth run amuck."

"I like it," he says, stepping closer into my space. I feel my own body incline toward his. "I think it's adorable."

"Adorable like toddler-adorable?"

"Adorable as in you make me laugh. You're beautiful, too." He reaches up with his free hand and tucks my hair behind my ear, then runs the length through his fingers.

I put my hand on his chest, bracing it there because I want to touch him, too. I'm met with one-hundred percent muscle. Somehow, though, I can feel his heartbeat thrumming wildly. I'm glad he's just as nervous as I am, even if he's better at hiding it.

"You look handsome, too."

I'm not sure which one of us takes a step back first. Disappointment at leaving his closeness, I let out a breath. While I would have longed to spend longer in his arms, but,, I'd bet good money Arthur, Marilyn or Shirley has the perfect view of us from their apartment and Aunt Isla's camped out at their window watching.

He goes to open the door and this time it's a success, no hands harmed in action. I get in and buckle myself, but he doesn't shut my door.

"I should mention now, car rides with me can be difficult." He leans against the door, ever the king of leaning and looking perfect. He taps scarred ear. "I'm deaf in this ear, so with you in the passenger seat, I can't hear much. You'll have to talk loud." For some reason, he looks a little embarrassed about his disability. I think he's more bothered I'll have to deal with it, than he is about having to live with it. "Sorry."

I reach out and take his hand again. I smile at him. It's nice to be the one with the higher ground for once. "It's fine—*you're* fine."

"Some people get a little fed up with it," he says. By some people, I wonder if he means past girls he's gone out with. I don't want to compare myself to them when I'm the one with him right now and they're not, but it's hard not to think about what those dates meant to *him*. It's horrible of people to make him feel self-conscious about something he can't help.

"When I'm nervous, I don't have a filter," I tell him. I tilt my head, willing him to look at me; he does. "Everyone has something that makes them unique. So if my mouth makes me adorable, your ear makes you brave."

34

His back straightens. "The world would be a better place if everyone spoke their mind."

"And the world would also be a better place if everyone accepted everyone's differences."

His eyes dilate and for a split second, I expect him to kiss me. I *want* him to. Who cares if we're in a parking lot? His gaze falls to my lips and I focus on keeping my breathing steady and not passing out. I'll bet he's a world-class kisser. If he's "handsome like Cary Grant," I bet he kisses with all the passion of a black and white movie.

Only he doesn't kiss me. Instead he shuts the door and walks around the Jeep to get in. I let out a rush of air and squeeze my eyes shut, a total ball of frustrated and missed opportunities. I think I hear him curse in a low tone just before he takes his seat. *Me too, bud, me too.* There's a similar string of curses going through my mind I would never say for fear my dad's ears will start burning.

When he backs up the car and pulls out on the main road, taking the same direction as the bus did, I decide it's time to woman-up and get over all my fears. He may be cute, but if there's one thing I can do, it's talk. Not that I'm *good* at talking, but just that I'm capable of it.

"My aunt mentioned you're deaf in one ear," I explain, trying to talk louder than usual.

He turns his head slightly to hear me, but still keeps his full concentration on the road. "Probably something else to make you think I was old."

"Yeah," I say a little too quietly. I raise my voice. "I still can't believe I thought that."

He shrugs. "It makes sense." I can't help but notice he's talking a little louder, too. I guess the acoustics are a little off in here for him. "I enlisted in the army when I was eighteen and about a year and a half ago, my unit was in a village when a bomb went off. They say I'm lucky to have hearing in my other ear and the scarring wasn't worse."

The scars on his body aren't the only scars he's sure to carry. A sweet, smiling, and kind man doesn't really pair with *army* and *bomb* in my mind. I guess you hear so much about the casualties of serving in the military, you forget some people come out better than they were going in...or at least stronger. His hearing might have been damaged, but not his heart or his resilience.

Thoughts barrage my mind, making it hard to come up with a good follow-up comment. I want it to matter. He's opening up to me about his history, so I should follow up with something equally meaningful, but compared to him, I don't think I've really lived.

"I think you're lucky you made it home with your spirit." I'm not sure if he hears me or if I want him to. "How did you come to work at a retirement home?"

"I grew up here. My parents passed away in a car accident when I was about three and I was sent here to live with grandpa. He passed right before I enlisted."

"I'm sorry about your parents and your grandpa."

"Thanks, Hope. It's something I've had to work through, but I realized along the way no matter what you believe in, you can't deny they're still with you." He smiles at me, as if to show me he's okay, while he waits for a red light to turn green. "I started doing stuff around the retirement home when I was in my teens—repairing things, mowing the lawn, doing whatever I could to earn my keep. I'm not sure I was even technically allowed to stay with him. When I enlisted in the army, I wanted to see the world and experience something outside of a retirement home. But the second I was discharged, I came back here. I realized this is my home and the residents are my family, you know? So they hired me and let me have one of the apartments." He sighs as we start moving again. "What does it say about me if I like living there?"

"That you have an old soul?" I offer. I'm not sure where he's taking me, which I probably should've clarified up front. If Paul weren't such an upstanding guy, I could be a *48 Hours* victim. I don't have the heart to ask now. I watch as we pass the grocery store we were at earlier, heading away from the commercial part of town. "I think it's nice you know where you want to be."

"Yeah. The army showed me the world, but I just wanted to come back here." He pulls onto a small patch of concrete off the road, where there's a little building designed to look like a sundae complete with a cherry on top. It's surround by nothing except sand and the ocean. It's so picturesque, it's romantic. "This is the best place for ice-cream in the area. Figured we could eat some then walk on the beach."

"Sounds perfect."

"Wait there a second," he says and winks at me.

He gets out and walks around the Jeep to open the door for me. "Thank you," I whisper. It's almost embarrassing how little experience I have with outright kindness. Nowadays, the idea of a southern gentleman seems closer to a fairy-tale.

We get in a several-families-deep line leading up to the window. This place is definitely a hot spot.

"You don't sound like you know where you want to be," he points out. He brings his hand up to squeeze his neck. "Not to offend."

I have the urge to reach up and grab his arm to comfort him. He doesn't seem the nervous type, which throws me off. "No, you're right," I admit. "I'm just at this crossroads. I'm bored, but I'm also comfortable—and it's hard to decide which one I'd rather break free from."

"That feeling led me to the army," he agrees. "I made the big jump, but maybe you should just try exploring your boundaries."

"Coming here was supposed to test my boundaries," I tell him. The trip was supposed to encourage me to get out of the house and visit somewhere new. I didn't expect to meet a guy.

It dawns on me no matter how much I like Paul, this will never really be more than two weeks. Maybe we'll go out on another date or maybe we won't, but I'll eventually go home and he'll stay here. My heart is betraying me by fluttering and pulling me toward him, because I can't give it to him. First date or not, I already know this won't amount to anything.

#

Our conversation lightens while we eat our ice cream cones. I tell him about my parents and Chloe. When I talk about Sam, Paul assures me he used to hide away, too.

"Boys are weird. I was just dramatic," I tell him, giving him a window to my teenage years—not that they're far behind.

He laughs, but doesn't say anything.

"Okay, maybe I still am."

"You have a way of making things...interesting," he says. He sounds as though he genuinely likes it. I'm glad someone does. I'm too busy wanting to bury my head in the sand.

I lean my elbows on the table, staring at my cone where the ice cream is beginning to melt and ooze down the sides. Probably not appropriate to lick at it. "I meant dramatic in the world-is-ending-sense. Not where I blurt random things out."

"Interesting in a good way, Hope. I'm used to honesty. All my life people pretty much say whatever—it was that way in the retirement home and in the army." He finishes his cone and the scrunches up his napkin to wipe as his mouth. "It's nice to have it, you know? It's a constant."

I nod, even though I don't really know what he means. My world is always the same, so I don't need a constant. I finish up my cone and go to throw away my napkin. When I turn back, he's standing and looking out at the beach.

"Ready for our walk?" he asks.

I answer him by starting toward the beach. I look over my shoulder at him, hoping my smile is somewhere close to as bright as his. He jogs to catch up, masterfully navigating the sandy parts like he was born here or something. I have to slow down, nearly tripping over my own feet. I stop, slip my sandals off and carry them. My toes slide into the deliciousness of the cold sand.

He surprises me by doing the same thing. Evidently his feet were going au natural, in his brown shoes. *Ouch.* He catches me watching and shrugs. "If you've had to walk as much as I've had to, your feet can withstand about anything," he explains. Personally, I don't believe him. This might be his one and only flaw.

We walk along the edge of the ocean so every once in a while it creeps up and submerges our feet. The water manages to catch me by surprise and make me gasp, each time. Even if the water "granted wishes," there was also a dangerous mysticism around it. As though it would rise up and pull you into its dark depths at a moment's notice. As much as the water gives, it can also take.

I laugh as a wave licks at my ankles then jumps up my leg. Paul chuckles, too, watching me closely. "Do you even notice any of this anymore? The ocean, I mean?" I question.

He turns my question over in his mind for a second. "Sometimes. Not before I left for the army, but when I came back, yeah."

"I don't think I'd ever get tired of this."

"I don't think you would, either," he agrees.

His hand brushes against mine and for a second, I pretend it's gravity, the wind, or some sort of invisible person. It's easier to believe in all of those things than to believe he's going to hold my hand. There have been times where I've thought something was going to happen and nothing. His hand brushes mine a second time, except his fingers link through mine, followed by a suave move and he's holding my hand completely. Something so small shouldn't make my whole arm tingle, shooting a bolt of lightning straight from my hand to my heart. I bite my lip, trying to tamper down the wave of giddiness overtaking me.

Paul doesn't even bother trying to hide whatever he's feeling, because he beams down at me. Dear Lord, I hope he's not laughing at me.

"What brought you here, anyway?" he asks.

"Well, there was this guy I met in a grocery store who wasn't old *at all*..."

"There you go again," he says rolling his eyes.

"Sorry," I say with a grin. I take a step closer into him, maybe his smile means he likes me as much as I like him. I slip my arm across my middle and hold his arm. We're alone on a huge patch of beach, but I can't get close enough to him. I've never felt so intimate with someone—romantic or otherwise. "I guess I'm sort of running."

"There's a big difference between running *away* and running *toward* something, you know," he points out. "You can do them both at the same time, too. So what are you doing?"

I blink half a dozen times. Paul's about thirty miles passed my speed limit; he knows a thing or two about life. I know exactly zip.

"Both, I think. Everyone I knew was hitting some huge milestone, while I...wasn't. I guess I just wanted to experience *something*."

He raises his free hand and snaps. "And a retirement home seemed like the best place to do that in."

"Hey, Aunt Isla and her friends lead a more exciting life than most people I know."

"Yeah, I shouldn't joke because it's true. Make fun of it all I want, but there's more experiences there than anyone can count. Years' and years' worth."

"It's almost like a time machine."

"That's exactly how it is. When I first came home, it was easier having some of the veterans to talk to. Even though they served in different wars, it's all guns and ammo and foreign soil." He huffs out a laugh, giving me a look. "I'm done talking about that—it's not a first date conversation."

"What exactly classifies first date conversations?"

"Colors, favorite foods, childhood pets, favorite movies."

"Yellow. I like cobbler, steak, fruit salads, any food— basically. We didn't have any pets, because my dad has allergies. And my favorite movie is *Psycho,* not that it's indicative of my personality."

"Well, if it is, we're alone on the beach and now's your chance, Norman Bates."

"No shower." I purposefully bump into him. "We're done with first date talk now, so we're free to talk about anything."

"Yeah, but you don't know mine," he says.

I've never done drugs, but I doubt the feeling would measure up to the euphoric, intoxicating rush he puts my body through.

As we walk for hours in a time span which feels only seconds long, we ask each other ridiculous questions. I laugh harder than I ever have. Somehow, I learn as much about myself as I learn about him.

I realize I've spent too much time waiting for this. Like with Aunt Isla, maybe you don't rush love, but let it happen when it wants.

The only problem is, waiting for it isn't going to be the problem anymore. It'll be leaving it.

#

"So...this is me, which I guess you know," I say as we approach the door to Aunt Isla's apartment.

He sighs as he leans against the wall. "You're definitely one for saying just about everything, including the obvious."

"It's a gift. I'm sorry I'm so awkward, I'm just—"
"Nervous?"
"Every day of my life," I say with a weird laugh.

"Tell me what you're nervous about?"

"Why would I do that?" I ask.

"Because you're honest, remember?"

"Oh, yeah. I need to invest more time into becoming a liar." I lean against the door, too. This is the part where I wish I could be one of those confident girls who take control of the situation. I want him to kiss me for real, instead of the fake out from before. But this little voice inside my head (and by little, I really mean gigantic) reminds me how embarrassing it would be for me to go in for the kill and get shot down. The imagery would be exactly how I would feel, too. "I guess I was just thinking about you...me...kissing..."

"'Sittin' in a tree,'" he sings off key. He leans into me. "Say no more." He cups my cheek as his lips brush against mine dangerously, yet sweet and slow. He still tastes like the banana ice cream he ate, mixed with something which reminds me of the ocean. I brace my hand against his chest, because I feel as if I'm going to sink right into him and just disappear completely into this kiss. This would be the good way to wind up on *48 Hours*.

But then my lips part and the kiss deepens. One of us—or maybe it's a mutual—sighs and my heart speeds up into cardiac arrest territory. His kiss is a rush of adrenaline and emotions, but I'm also completely aware of everything between the two of us, from the way his lips feel against mine to how he's gently stroking my cheeks with his fingertips.

He pulls back from me and rests his forehead against mine. We're both breathing like we ran a marathon.

"Woah, huh?" I say, continuing with the can't-keep-my-mouth-shut thing.

He doesn't say anything, just lets out a long breath and nods. *Then* leans in to kiss me again. This time, there's more behind it. Not so gentle and more like he's kissed me a thousand times already and plans to do it a thousand times more. He kisses me as if he already has a trademark on my heart and knows it. I've always thought too much while I kissed someone—how I should move my lips, where my hands should go, if I should close my eyes. But right now, I can't think. The instinct to *be* with him in this moment has taken over and my body isn't doing anything except reacting. So *this* is how I'm supposed to feel.

SMACK.

"Arthur, they probably heard you!"

"Well now that you yelled at me, I'm sure they did!"

I break away and pull back, but Paul only drops his hands to grip my waist.

"They must have been watching us through the peep hole," I point out.

Paul shifts, so I'm closer to his other ear. I must be hard to hear. My voice seems quieter to my own ears. And breathy. "Probably just Isla. I'll bet Arthur was trying to stop her."

"This means I'm going to be mortified for the rest of this trip."

He laughs. "She was probably cheering us on. No need to be mortified."

"Embarrassed?"

"No."

"Scarred?"

He shakes his head, looking exasperated, but somehow happy about it. "Try something a little more positive, huh?"

I roll my eyes. "Fine. She'll probably be excited and it'll rub off on me."

#

Somehow, our ice-cream date turns into another date. Only it's not really a date. He tricks me into thinking it was a date by using the phrase, "come spend some time with me." Really, he was dragging me off from apartment to apartment and around the grounds to help out with

43

manual labor.

"It's not a date you're looking for," I say for the millionth time. "It's an apprentice."

Sure, he hasn't made me work *that* much—he's really just had me sit there and talk to him—but when I have helped him, I've realized the only reason why he's strong enough for this job is because he was used to it. Me, in my black tank top and khaki cut offs, with my hair pulled up in a high ponytail— not so much. I'm dying of over-exhaustion.

Okay, a little dramatic, I know. But I seriously helped him carry a resident's new couch up to their apartment. It's no easy task for a girl who can't reach the *barely* tall shelves at a store.

Paul gives me a sly smile as he takes the hammer from my hand to hammer a nail in the wall. We're hanging pictures for Marilyn, because Shirley wants her to have more mementos to remind her of her life. Watching them has taught me about another form of love—the friendship kind of love. The kind where you dedicate a piece of your heart to protect someone, care for them, and expect them to always be there for you. It makes me want to call Chloe and apologize for being a horrible best friend, because I want to be the Marilyn to her Shirley or vice-versa.

"So what if I want to see you more *and* make my job a little easier?" he asks.

"You're good at the talking part." I sit on the arm of the couch he's using as a pseudo-ladder. "But your action leaves little to be desired."

"You really think that?" he asks, sounding as confident as ever, lips curling up into a knowing grin.

"That kiss doesn't count."

"Somehow me *asking* you to help me carry a couch into a room makes me the bad guy."

"Exactly." I fluff the tendrils escaping my ponytail indignantly "Besides, you knew I'd agree because I want to show you I don't just babble endlessly and can actually be useful."

"You ain't gotta prove anything," he says, hanging one of the pictures on the nails. He steps back off the couch, like he's part-ninja, and moves toward me.

He effortlessly positions himself between my legs and places his hands on my thighs. It's almost scary how easily he does it—as though we've known each other longer than we have. More amazing is I *let* him. Like I'm experienced at hanging out with him or we're a couple or something.

Oh my god, we're dating. I'm "together" with a guy.

He leans in and kisses me, our bodies curving into each other. The kissing feels frenzied now we're far away from prying eyes and peepholes. Not too alone, though, because we're in Marilyn's apartment. Still, I can't stop my arms from rising up his body and winding around his neck. My fingers instantly find the scars on his neck, leading up to his ear.

His skin immediately heats there and he deepens the kiss, as if he enjoys how I'm willing to touch him where he feels broken. Not that he should feel that way—I think he's beautiful for what he's been through.

#

The next week is a montage of kissing, laughing, talking, and helping Paul around the retirement home. The time I meant to spend with Aunt Isla or lazing around on the beach, is spent with him. I barely see Aunt Isla except for at night and in the morning, or when we're in her apartment doing something.

Paul receives so many calls for him to fix things, he keeps his phone on silent; there's something other-worldly in how easily things go awry here. One of the tenants believes there's something wrong with her thermostat and we return to her apartment daily. There's nothing wrong, of course. Instead, Paul just messes with it like he's fixing it and somehow convinces her it's better, which she believes whole heartedly until the next day. His patience and kindness with everyone amazing, even though, I'm sure the neediness can be tiring. He really loves and enjoys his work and the people. Clearly they love him as well, because Paul comes away from every apartment with either a kiss, hug or a handshake and some kind of sweet treat, which we share out on the beach.

Today we're eating a piece of coconut creme pie, a piece of golden heaven. I take a fork-full bigger than my mouth and shove it inside, which isn't very ladylike. Luckily, Paul's doing the same. There's something special between us if we can eat like barbarians together.

He looks at me, mid-chew, and we both start laughing. You'd think we're eating our last meal.

I swallow and take a sip of the peach tea we stole from Aunt Isla's refrigerator.

"Endless chatter time. If I could do one thing for the rest of my life shamelessly and guilt free, I would just eat and not care about my weight, my skin, or socialization." I look up at him, trying to muster my best straight face. "I'd go full on grizzly bear."

"You never cease to surprise me, Hope," he chuckles. He bumps his shoulder against mine. He's carefully balancing our pie on his kneecap, like he does with all the other sweets. The man could start break dancing and still manage to keep it from falling into the sand. His best quality is his devotion to keeping food safe. "I'd just lay on the beach all day, sun be damned."

"What about the water? You'd be a prune, so that ought to be damned too, you know."

"Hey, I didn't knock your bear plan."

"Which was very kind."

He raises his eyebrows but doesn't say anything.

"Fine, I'm sorry."

"You sound a little put out."

"Sorry."

He sighs and sets the plate in my lap. "Have the rest of

this."

"What? Why? I really am sorry—"

"No, it's not that. I guess, I just...uh," he says, trailing off. He brings his hand up to scratch his chin. I momentarily lose all thought and focus as the muscles in his arm dance. "We've only got a few days left, don't we?"

I suddenly lose my appetite, too. "What brought this up?"

"I don't know. Just thinking I'm going to miss this."

"Me being overly chatty?"

"That, yeah."

"And how I'm your unpaid helper?"

"Yeah."

"But you're really just going to miss *me* in general, right? The most?"

He turns his head to look at me. "The most."

I can't help but want to kiss him. Somehow, I manage to catch him off guard and tackle him to the ground. Another fail at being the initiator. He takes it with grace— not as if I just attacked him. He shifts my legs to his sides so they're aligned with his hips and I'm basically sitting on him, then tucks my hair behind my ears.

"The most," he repeats again and pulls me down for a long, tangled kiss that makes my heart race and parts of my body heat up in the most extraordinary way, until I'm writhing against him like I'm trying to win a race. Better yet, so is he. This is the farthest we've gone and I'm not sure if it's because he senses I'm not ready for more or if it's because he wants it to stay at a sweet, heart-stopping summer romance. The kind you imagine they were singing about in *Grease*.

#

"Shirley, please. Nobody wants to know about the wonders of modern medicine," Arthur groans, hands over his face.

"I'm telling you, it was wonderful," Shirley sing songs, nudging Marilyn, who only gives her a sweet smile in return.

I don't need to hear the entire conversation to know they're talking about something scandalous I definitely don't want to think about. I mean, good for them having sex at their age, but bad for me. The horrific images should remain a secret forever.

Luckily, Arthur notices me sitting down at their table and clears his throat. I give him a grateful smile.

"Oh, she's old enough to hear these things," Shirley says.

"You have to be over eighty to hear what you're talking about, Shirley," Aunt Isla points out. "If she hears it now, she'll have a permanent fear of sex and growing old."

Shirley pouts her red lips. "Viagra and other enhancement drugs are perfectly acceptable in today's society. I don't see why it's so bad for her to hear about their wonders."

"I'm sure you're right, but you go into detail. *Too* much detail," Aunt Isla says, with an enough-is-enough tone. Little does she know while I was waiting for the elevator yesterday Shirley already educated me about Viagra and her sex life. My brain feels like it went through the blender with lemons. "So, to what do we owe this honor of you joining us?"

"Hey, you wanted this," Arthur huffs at Isla.

I blush. "I just thought I should have breakfast with you all since I'll be leaving soon."

"Paul could've joined," Aunt Isla says. Her mockingly formal attitude gone.

"I know, but he's getting some work done so he can have the afternoon free."

"How sweet," she says dreamily. "I'm so glad the two of you like each other. I knew you two would be perfect. Do you have plans for after you leave?"

"No, we haven't talked about it."

"But you're going to right?"

"Yes," I promise. I couldn't sleep last night thinking about our future. He must have been having the same issue because I got a text from him at four this morning. He said he wasn't ready for us to end and wanted to talk.

Shirley claps her hands across from us. "I'm so happy for you."

My face gets hotter. "Me too." The urge to say, *I like him, I really like him*, overwhelms me.

"You're a catch, dear," Aunt Isla says, while Arthur mimics reeling in a fish. It makes me snort and earns Arthur a slap on the hand from Isla, followed by a kiss on the cheek.

"Definitely," Shirley agrees. "There's a reason why no one else stuck. They weren't you."

My ears perk. "No one else?"

Aunt Isla pales as she shakes her head. "She just means his other girlfriends."

I blink a few times. Why does she seem like she's lying? "I don't think that's what Shirley means."

"Oh, it is," Shirley says quickly.

I raise an eyebrow.

"You can't lie to the girl," Arthur grumbles. "It's unfair to her."

Aunt Isla looks down at her breakfast, moving her eggs around with her fork. She won't meet my gaze. "Paul tends to date a lot of girls—we all set him up with one of our own. It's sort of a ritual."

"I set my niece up with him before he went overseas," Shirley adds, like it helps or something.

"So... so this has happened before?" I stutter.

"Not exactly—not like—" Aunt Isla starts, but I don't hear the rest.

Her words get lost on their journey to my ears. I'm just one of many? He's spent his other summers with other girls? Seeing them in the same way he's been seeing me? I mean, I assumed he's dated, but not in the same way as he's been seeing me.

I feel wrong—like I'm just part of an endless revolving door of summer flings. I was having this rare moment with shooting stars and wishes come true, but really, I'm closer to a pattern piece. Of course, our relationship means more to me than it does to him. It's my first special, real romance. To him, I'm just a date in a list longer than I'm willing to guess.

I thought my life back home was boring. Boring beats mortifying.

What am I doing here?

My body feels as though I'm falling head first into a volcano. Lava, galore. Tears brim my eyes and I'm half-surprised steam doesn't rise. I tuck my chin down because I know I won't be able to hide them. Instead, I mumble something about needing to go for a walk.

They're all nimble for their age, but none are fast enough to keep up with me. I bolt out of the door and run for the stairwell, which is used for emergencies only. All I want is a minute alone.

Okay, a minute to wallow.

I should've stuck to the original plan of spending time with Aunt Isla and going to the beach. The safe experience I wanted and planned for. Then handsome, dream-guy Paul had to show up with fudge. He kissed me like they do in the movies and cherished me like they talk about in books. He had to say sweet things and make me invested in him. He made me want things. I questioned why I couldn't stretch two weeks out further. Most of all, he had to go and make me want *more,* which I obviously can't have. Why did he make me believe the magic was real?

I run my palm over my nose, despite the ugly noise and slickness that comes with the movement. So what if I'm gross and dramatic? This is real. This is anguish .

Well, I had an experience all right. The first time my heart broke. I don't think I'll compare my paint to anything in the past again, because they're all meaningless compared to this.

My phone buzzes in my pocket and I take it out. Who could be calling? Thankfully, it's my best friend in the entire world.

I answer the phone with a sniffle. "Hi, Chloe."

"Hope?" she asks, tentatively. "Are you okay? You sound sad."

I choke on a sob. "I'm so stupid."

"No, you're not. You're the opposite. Do I need to call up a hitman?"

I laugh, but it feels pathetic and more like a gasp for air. "Call the hit on *me*, please."

"Not someone else?"

"No." I squeeze my eyes shut. "I'm the asinine one."

"Why?"

"Because, there was a guy."

"That's usually the beginning to a fairytale or a tragedy."

"This was a tragedy. Like, a full on Shakespeare-kills-everybody tragedy."

She snorts. "Well, then, who are the players?"

"Me."

"And?"

My chest tightens. "Paul."

I don't say anything for a while, but then the words flow. I tell her everything, from our first meeting to just now. I apologize for not mentioning him sooner. I just didn't want to get her hopes up. It's happened before for guys who weren't nearly as promising. Even more, *I* didn't want to be disappointed. What if we both got our hopes up...then nothing?

"I'm sorry I've been a bad best friend," I finish.

"Nope, you don't get to say that. Not when you're hurting. When my girl's heart is broken, we build it back up, not tear it down."

#

My things are tucked neatly in my bag when someone knocks, then bangs, on Aunt Isla's door. I called my mom, too, and we decided I should come home a day sooner. Isla gives me a questioning glance, as she has with all of the texts and calls I've ignored from him.

"Please, Hope, I know you're in there."

I freeze in the middle of flatting down my things. His voice even hurts to hear.

"Isla called me."

I immediately pin her with a glare. "I thought you were on my side," I whisper-yell at her.

"I only want what's best for you," she says. "Which includes forcing you to face the hard things. You need to talk to him."

I tuck my hair behind my ears. I have it braided sloppily, but it's falling down, basically the same chaos I'm in. "You're a turncoat, you know?"

She laughs, loud enough for Paul to hear. "Take it from me, you'll be happy I've done this. Life is too long of a sentence for missed opportunities." She walks up beside me and places her hand on my cheek. "I love you like a granddaughter. I hope you know that."

I place my hand over hers. "I love you, too. I'm sorry for being this way."

"I was wreck when it came to love and then I had Arthur. You're allowed to be a wreck. Just find yourself faster, dear. Whether it means you're meant for love or not."

"This isn't love with Paul."

"You're acting like it, honey," she says. "But these old eyes sometimes see things that aren't there." She looks at the clock on the mantel of her fireplace. "Now, Arthur and I have knitting class in a few minutes, so the door is going to open."

"Okay." As much as I hate it, talking to Paul is probably for the best. I don't want to look back on this for the rest of my life as something I didn't do.

She kisses me on the cheek and goes to the door. When she opens it, Paul looks shocked, but recovers himself quickly. For the first time since meeting him, he's not smiling. He's pale, with his lips drawn in a tight, grim line, and unable to meet my eyes. There's a dribble of cream paint on his cheeks, with larger blots on his clothes.

Aunt Isla whispers something in his good ear before walking by him and down the hall. He steps inside the apartment and closes the door behind him.

"Isla called me and told me what happened," he says, voice raspy.

"I wish she wouldn't have." I look down at my bare feet.

"Yeah, me too. I wish you'd have heard it from me." A small piece of me hoped they were wrong. His words prove I was the only one who was in the dark. He comes closer, which makes me step away reflexively. He winces, but reaches for my bag to zip it for me. "What are you thinking, Hope?"

"I've never felt special, but you made me feel like I am. And I thought...but I'm not... really, am I?" Tears well up, but I blink them away. The last thing I want to do is turn into a sobbing mess. I wish I could do the same for my mouth. "Do you have a side of things to tell? Or are you so calm because I'm right?" I mess with the tip of my braid to hide my anxiety at hearing him say the words. "I know I'm being weird about this and probably not reacting right."

"You're not being weird," he tells me. "It's fair what you're feeling. I was going to tell you about the others, but I didn't know how to—didn't exactly want to talk about it, either." He finishes zipping my backpack and faces the couch. "Can we, ah, sit down?"

"Yeah." I point to the couch. "How about I get a towel, though?" I quickly get one out of the bathroom and set it on the couch so he can sit down. I curl up at the end, as far away from him as I can get.

He stares at me for a long time, like he's searching my face for his next sentences. Doubtful. "Everyone here is family to me and they all want to make me a *real* family member. Before I went overseas, I couldn't get a date to save my life. I think girls thought the old-timers were contagious or something. So everyone set me up with the girls who would come to town. After a while, I realized that wasn't working either, but I couldn't turn anyone down. When I came back home, it was worse. It felt like I had a new date every other week, but nothing stuck. They all wanted the war-hero, but not the damaged goods that come with it." He looks away, his gaze going somewhere else entirely. "Then I saw you—got to know you—and, Hope, you *are* special."

I feel stupid for using the word *special*. What does that even mean—special? I wring my hands in my lap. "I'm so sorry. I'm overreacting. We haven't even known each other very long."

"You're not," he assures me. He reaches for my hand and tugs on it gently. Once our fingers lace together, he pulls me toward him. I come willingly, until our thighs are pressed together and my head is on his shoulder.

"I just always feel so behind, but then I met you and I thought I was on the right page. I found out about the other girls and I was behind again," I explain.

He kisses the top of my head, his lips lingering there. "You're not behind. I'm in the same place you are. Believe it or not, the way I feel is new to me, too."

"Really?"

"Yeah. I've always thought I was destined to be an eighty-year old bachelor, probably still living here. And then you came along. Now I'm hoping..."

My mouth drops and I pull away to see if he's serious. "You're kidding."

"I'm not."

I catch him off guard by kissing him, but he quickly

catches on and starts kissing me back. "I think you're my soul mate," I say against his lips. "Old souls and all."

He chuckles. "Who knew my fear would be the thing to thaw you out."

"I realize I'm not the only person in the world who feels this way, but it's nice to *be* with somebody who does." I grin at him. "It makes the future seem less scary."

"Why? So we can be lonely together?" he jokes and I elbow him in the ribs. "I know what you meant."

Seriousness washes over me at the idea of us being together in any sense. "So where does this leave us?"

"It's been on my mind for a while. I'm not ready for what's going on between us to end, but I know it's time for you to leave—even if it's sooner than we thought." He tucks my hair behind my ear and I automatically reach up to run my thumb along the crevasse of his dimple. "I want us to keep seeing each other and talking to each other. Exclusively, obviously. But I also know I want you to go home and think hard about *your* future. Not *ours*. I think it's important you realize what you want. Like I said, this place is my home, so I want you to think about where your home is."

"You sound like a teacher, not a boyfriend."

"It happens when you live with old folks," he says. "Am I making sense, though?"

"You are. I agree. I need to find myself first." This time I know I won't be able to stop my tears. I bury myself in his chest, before continuing in a rush, "Thank you, Paul. I'm finally on track with where I want to be and it's all because of you."

"No, you took the chance. I just happened to be here."

"I'm not sure what I thought I was looking for this summer, but this is it."

#

A year later, Chloe and her *very*-soon-to-be-husband say

their vows, saying words I didn't really understand until Paul. I watch Chloe enjoy the happiest moment of her life since this is the instant we've been gushing about for months. I've been excited to see the love in their eyes, to see them both cry, and witness the beginning of their forever. Basically, all the gooey stuff I never thought I'd be able to face without being jealous.

Except, instead of looking at them, I search the audience for *my* guy. This is the first time he's visited my hometown. Normally, we meet halfway or I stay with Aunt Isla. There was a wreck on the highway, so I was disappointed when I got the text saying he would be late. We had been planning for him to come see me before the wedding, but instead he had to go straight to my house to catch a ride to the church with my family.

Even though I knew he made it here thanks to a text, I think I would've felt his presence no matter what. The second I started walking down the aisle, my arm linked with the best man's, chill bumps rose and my heart pounded. Being in the same room with him still turns me into a wreck of emotions and reactions. He's sitting on the end of the four-person row next to my dad. When I passed, he reached for my hand and kissed it, giving me his signature lopsided grin.

He still smiling now, but differently—like he's thinking the same way as me and imagining us someday up at the altar. Then again, it could be a signal I'm picking up from my mom.

After I talked and talked and *talked* about Paul, my family rented a beach house near Isla's retirement home. My mom instantly loved him and seemed to have our entire life planned out—not that I hadn't done so already. Sam, who morphed from Teenage-Shut-In to Mr. Outgoing in the blink of an eye, hero-worships Paul. The person I was most worried about was my dad, but he instantly clicked with him, too. My dad even sometimes calls him if he has questions about something he's trying to fix, since Dad's lost when it comes to that stuff.

When the ceremony ends, I walk back down the aisle, my legs as loose as putty. Even though I talk to Paul almost every day, seeing him still unnerves me. For three weeks, we couldn't see each other with our schedules out of whack.

Our long distance thing isn't working, even if we're as close as ever, so I really hope he understands my decision.

We're ushered into a small room to wait for pictures, which ends up being fun and a little nostalgic when Chloe and I get solo ones. I want this night to drag out in a good way for my best friend, but I'm also ready for it to speed up so I can spend time with Paul. Seeing Chloe so happy and in love, makes me want what she has.

I do love Paul. We haven't formally said it to each other, which is weird because most my friends say it in like month two. It's what makes our relationship more important and special. We aren't rushing anything because we want to be sure.

He did say it one night, when it was late and we didn't get to talk until about one in the morning—way passed when we both usually go to sleep. He fell asleep talking to me, right before murmuring those three words. I spent the whole night rehashing them, going from one extreme where I was elated, to another where I figured I was hearing things. It didn't make matters any better because neither of us mentioned it again.

Then, about a month ago, I was so excited to see him I said it in a rush, only I said it in his deaf ear.

After the pictures, the MC of the night announces the bridal party so we can make our entrance into the reception all. I hold my bouquet up and do a little dance, but as soon as the spotlight's off of me, strong arms wrap around my middle and warm lips press against the crook of my neck.

I wrap mine around his neck and turn my face to see his side profile. He's clean-shaven, which makes his skin feel softer than ever against mine. Admittedly, I still love his scarred parts the most. I love kissing and touching him there and reminding him how I find him handsome not only in the way he looks, but also in his courage.

Not everyone decides to put their life in danger by defending their country because they set out to find themselves.

"I missed you," he says against my skin, chills rise like an army ready for battle.

"I missed you, too. I'm so glad you came."

"I told you I would—I remember *promising*," he says, chuckling.

"And, you're always right." I turn around in his embrace and lean back to get a look at him. He's wearing a fitted gray suit with a white shirt underneath unbuttoned at the collar, showing off his beach worthy tan. Most importantly, he's wearing his ever-present grin and staring at me like I'm the only girl in the world.

"You're perfect, Hope," he says and runs his hand down the side of my face. "You look beautiful."

I blush and fight the urge to run my hands down the soft fabric of my dress. I love the fit and feel like I *am* beautiful, something I haven't really felt since Aunt Isla made me over. But, at the same time, I also keep stressing about the dark purple color clashing with my hair, which seems exceptionally bright against it.

Confidence, Hope. Confident people make big decisions, so it's time to step up to the challenge. My hair, my mind, my life is on the right track, even if it's not always easy to see.

I link my hand through his, letting it lay with his on my cheek for a minute as I gather up my courage. "I want to show you something."

"Right now?" he asks. "Don't you have duties to do?" He looks around, but the rest of the party has scattered. The new Mr. and Mrs. are even at opposite ends of the room talking to people.

"Yes, right now." *Before I lose my courage again.* I had

meant to talk to him when we'd last met, but I wimped out. It's now or never, since my plans basically go into place tomorrow.

I pull him behind me out toward the parking lot, where my car has been sitting all day long.

"Is this the part where you murder me for all my worldly possessions?" he asks. "I don't have a will, babe. So it ain't gonna work."

"Unless, I wrote up a fake." Joking with him eases my anxiety.

When we come to a stop behind my blue car, I look up at him, waiting for him to see it. He doesn't, of course. Instead he just stares at my car like he's seen it before and is completely lost.

"Sorry," he says, running a hand through his hair. "Care to share?"

I swallow. I have to point it out. This probably wasn't the best way to go about this. I point to the *new* little emblem, now in the corner of my rear window where my old university logo used to be. "I'm transferring."

"That's literally a half-hour away from the retirement home," he says evenly.

"Yeah..."

"Hope, are you saying...?"

I turn to him and say in a rush, "You said I needed to figure out myself and my home. I honestly worked at it this past year. But every day, I would end up looking forward to your calls, to the next time I would see you, to when we would get to spend more time together. I would leave anything and everything behind for you. *You're* my home, Paul. Wherever you are, I want to be. I never wanted to put myself out there because I was afraid to change or leave my comfort zone. But with you, I'm not. " I look up into his eyes, trying to convey the strength of the words I'm saying and everything in between. "I love you."

He's stoic and for a split second I think he's going to tell me he doesn't love me back. I'm used to a serious Paul.

But even though everything about him is still, I can see twenty million emotions swirling around in his eyes. It's as if he's feeling too much to show any of it.

Then, all of a sudden, he kisses me, transferring every single one of his emotions between our lips. I can feel the words he's trying to convey without having to hear them, because they've started to grow in my soul.

"I love you, too," he murmurs. He pulls back in a state of awe. "I'm your home."

"We'll just put a welcome mat at your feet."

He chuckles. "You're mine, too, you know. I probably would've moved if given the chance."

"I know, but you love it where you are and I love it there, also."

"They are our speed."

He pulls me into a hug, still laughing out of happiness and excitement for the future. With his deaf ear close to my lips, I say the words I'm ready for, but not sure if it's time for, "I wish to grow old with you."

SNEAK PEEK AT STEP TOWARD YOU

CHAPTER ONE

Silas

One: We admitted we were powerless over alcohol—that our lives had become unmanageable.

The alcohol is the first thing I smell. It always is. It's also the first thing I think about when I wake up, and the only thing on my mind for the rest of the day.

Beer is always my drink of choice when I'm alone, but when someone's near, it's always vodka. Clear, no smell, no one ever guesses it's on me. Tonight, though, I didn't go with either of those. I wanted whiskey. I wanted the burn of it as it rushed down my throat, infecting me. I wanted to forget yelling at my mom, how I'd called her something nasty and regrettable—and how it hadn't felt nasty at the time and I didn't regret it.

Two: Came to believe that a Power greater than ourselves could restore us to sanity.

The coppery taste in my mouth and the blood making it impossible to see are clear signs that this isn't just another morning after a binge. No, it's still night.

Three: Made a decision to turn our will and our lives over to the care of God as we understood Him.

A smattering of memories overtakes me. Drinking at the bar—the bartender cutting me off. Stumbling to the nearby liquor store and buying the bottle of whiskey from the wary-looking guy who probably considered calling the cops, but didn't. Then driving, then flying, then darkness. Now this.

Blood, alcohol, numbness, upside-down in the seat of my car.

Four: Made a searching and fearless moral inventory of ourselves.

There was another car.

Five: Admitted to God, to ourselves, and to another human being the exact nature of our wrongs.

I hit somebody.

Six: Were entirely ready to have God remove all these defects of character.

I hit somebody and I want another drink. I want to move, even though I know I'm bleeding, and I want to find the whiskey. I want to drown in it.

Seven: Humbly asked Him to remove our shortcomings.

Eight: Made a list of all persons we had harmed, and became willing to make amends to them all.

How many people were there in the car? *God, don't let them be dead.* What if there were kids? What if it was a family? What if it was old people? What if…

Nine: Made direct amends to such people wherever possible, except when to do so would injure them or others.

If I'm not dead, then they can't be dead. I should have died.

Ten: Continued to take personal inventory and when we were wrong, promptly admitted it.

I don't even know what I said to my mom, and it probably doesn't even matter because there's no way it outweighs all of the other shit I've done. I do remember telling my dad to fuck off, and giving him the finger, but he can take it. My mom—she can't, and she doesn't deserve to.

Eleven: Sought through prayer and meditation to improve our conscious contact with God as we understood Him, praying only for knowledge of His will for us and the power to carry that out.

If I hurt anyone, I want to die. I *hope* I die. It'll be the only way I'll stop drinking, because I don't have the strength to change.

Twelve: Having had a spiritual awakening as the result of these steps, we tried to carry this message to alcoholics, and to practice these principles in all our affairs.

Sirens, lights.

I'm not going to die.

Goddamn it.

***

Step One: We admitted we were powerless over alcohol-that our lives had become unmanageable.

There are twelve steps in Alcoholics Anonymous and Silas Manning knows all of them by heart. He's been living them since a drunk driving accident resulted in the destruction of three lives. When he meets Rooney Oliver, he quickly realizes you can be addicted to things other than alcohol—you can be addicted to people, too.

Rooney's mother is dying and Rooney feels like she's dying with her. It's not until Silas comes into their lives that any of them start feeling hope—but Silas isn't ready to let go of the past or open himself up to a future.

Sometimes the only person who you want to lose is yourself.

Available at all major retailers

SNEAK PEEK AT SORT OF NORMAL

CHAPTER ONE

Carter

My pseudo-stalker has no concept of the no-shirt, no-shoes, no-service rule.

He grins at me, showing off his wolfishly sharp teeth, as he places a bottled water in front of me so I can ring it up. He produces a wallet and leans against the counter, waiting.

My eyebrows raise as I give a pointed look at the sign that says in *bold, capitalized, underlined* font, "No Shirt, No Shoes, No Service." The sign has progressed in stages from a small, barely-readable reminder on the front door to what feels like a gigantic billboard by the cash register. I'm not sure what else to do but put the phrase in skywriting.

And this customer, Boone Fell, probably has some ambition to star on the reality TV show *Naked and Afraid*. Thank God he hasn't gone so far as to ditch his pants.

Yet.

"I stop here durin' my run, Carter," he says in a thunderous southern drawl I know better than my own voice. "What—do you want me to dehydrate?"

I don't answer him, because what I have to say isn't exactly appropriate. *Yes, I do want you to dehydrate. Preferably in clothes.* Granted, it's not the worst thing I could say, but I know it's enough to make my boss angry. He's never liked me on account of a one-night stand he once had with my mama, which probably went well up until she stole his TV to sell. I'm surprised he even hired me, but from what I've heard, the manager doesn't bother going to him with potential new hires. It's really no use, given how many people start working here and then quit.

"You're getting so crafty with that sign, Carter," Boone says, getting closer to inspect it. "You know, if you end up going to college, you should give some serious thought to a degree in marketing."

I know he's mocking me, but his words still catch me off guard. Somehow, he knows I've been thinking about not going to college.

"C'mon," he says, reading my mind, "I listen to the things I hear about you. I pay attention. I've gotta if I'm gonna keep track of your schedule. You know how hard it is to schedule my daily runs around you?"

I picture my heart with a chain-link fence around it— also barbed wire and electricity—as I level my gaze with his. I've known Boone Fell since I was in diapers, back when I used to live beside him, our trailers practically twins. Growing up, he was sweet, and it felt like he would move heaven or hell for me. For the longest time, he was the only dependable person I knew and maybe even the only person who cared about me more than drugs, alcohol, sex, and all of the other vices known to man. It was easy to love him then. It didn't help that his dimples were disarming yet innocent, that his now short hair was shaggy—which always made his blue eyes play peekaboo—and that he was sort of awkward in a gangly, young boy sense. Now, he's a man who knows how to use those dimples to get what he wants—the same with those eyes—and he's muscular, tall, and moves like a predator stalking its prey.

The problem is, I've known this version of Boone for long enough to recognize I'm his repeat prey; it never fails once he catches me, and he sort of just leaves me dying out in the sun. For Boone, the game he plays with me has always been about the chase. I wish I would've realized that sooner when he had more of me to catch.

"It'll be ninety-nine cents," I tell him in a most even voice. Some days, like today, I just try to ignore him. Other days, I snap back. No matter what I do, though, it wears me out. *He* tires me out.

He digs through his wallet for change. Only Boone would (a) not have a credit card and (b) want to give me the exact change rather than a dollar bill like most people.

"You know, I was wearing shoes. I put them outside the front door, because of our little inside joke here. I was also wearing socks, but I thought, *what the hell*, and decided to make my feet naked—free."

He carefully sets out nine dimes and starts into the pennies, clacking each against the counter. I don't know if he intentionally tries to be annoying and loud, but he's a pro at it.

"It's not an inside joke, Boone. It's a rule."

"She speaks!" he says, looking up at me. "I love your voice and personality, Junebug."

"Boone ..." I bite down on the side of my tongue; I've already said too much. It barely takes anything to egg him on. He's like a toy that you can crank up but can't stop.

When he's finished with his pennies, I feel his gaze roam over me. I can't look at him. Instead, I mess with my ugly blue work shirt. Since he started coming in, I've started resenting this shirt. I've also started paying more attention to my hair and actually doing my makeup. I shouldn't care as much as I do.

***

Falling in love isn't as easy as staying in love.

Carter Hart and Boone Fell's lives are tangle of perfect and imperfect memories. In a world of drugs, alcoholism and neglectful parents, their love for each other kept them strong. But all it takes is one kiss and a lie to tear them apart.

When Carter's brother, Declan, dies of an overdose, Boone decides he can't let another day of secrets and mistaken circumstances keep them apart. His only problem? Now that he's ready to move forward with Carter, she's ready to leave him where she thinks he belongs: in the past.

Available Where Books Are Sold…

ABOUT THE AUTHOR

Liz Ashlee is the author of *Step Toward You, Sort of Normal, and Heart's a Mess.* She received her M.A. in English from Northern Kentucky University. Liz currently resides in Independence, Kentucky, where she is living her happy ever after with her husband, dog, and cats.

Facebook: https://www.facebook.com/LizAshleeAuthor/

Twitter: https://twitter.com/LizAshleeAuthor

Instagram: https://www.instagram.com/LizAshleeAuthor/?hl=en

Website: http://liz-ashlee.com/